CASE of the MISSING CHICK

Written by Erica Frost

Illustrated by Paul Harvey

Troll Associates

Troll Associates, Mahwah, N.J.

Library of Congress Catalog Card Number: 78-18036
ISBN 0-89375-092-1

In a cozy cradle, on a nest of straw, Harriet Hen sat on her egg. It was almost time for the hatching to begin.

"Oh, joy!" clucked Harriet. "I can hardly wait to see my baby!"

After a while, the grandmother clock struck.

"Time for tea," sang Harriet, and hopped off her nest.

She fluttered into the kitchen, and opened the cupboard door. The tea jar was empty. Not a tea bag remained.

"Oh dear!" clucked Harriet. "I do so love my cup of tea. But if I hurry, surely I can get to the market and back before my egg hatches."

So she took her shopping basket, and hurried off to the market.

Harriet put some corn and a box of tea bags into her basket. Then she got on the checkout line behind her good friend, Polly Pig.

"Oh, Polly!" clucked Harriet. "Will you please change places with me? My egg is ready to hatch, and I am in a great hurry!"

"Of course," grunted Polly. She took her basket of truffles, and changed places with Harriet. "Call me when the chick arrives," she squealed. "I sewed the sweetest cover for its cradle."

"I will," promised Harriet.

She waited in line behind Gussie Goose.
The clock on the wall said twenty minutes
after eleven.

"Oh, Gussie!" clucked Harriet. "Will you
please change places with me? My egg is
ready to hatch, and I am in a great hurry!"

"Of course," honked the goose. She took her basket of apples, and changed places with Harriet. "Call me when the chick arrives," she smiled. "I crocheted the cutest booties for it."

"I will," promised Harriet.

She waited in line behind Harvey Horse.
The clock on the wall said twenty-five minutes
after eleven.

"Harvey, my friend," clucked Harriet,
"will you please change places with me? My
egg is ready to hatch, and I am in a great
hurry!"

"Of course," neighed the horse. He took his sack of oats, and changed places with Harriet. "Call me when the little one arrives," he whinnied. "I made a fine rocking rooster for it."

"I will," promised Harriet.

When it was her turn, Harriet paid for the tea bags and the corn. Then she thanked her friends, and waved goodbye.

Harriet hurried home as fast as she could.

She opened her door and went straight to the cradle.

It was empty! Not even a shell
remained!

"Oh, me! Oh, my!" cried Harriet Hen. "Where can my little chick be?"

She looked under the table and under the chairs. She looked in the cupboard and under the stairs. She flew in and out of every room.

"Junior!" she squawked. "Ju-u-u-unior! Where are you?"

No one answered.

"Someone has taken my egg!" she cried.
"Who could have done this dreadful deed?"
Harriet stood by the empty cradle and
cried as if her heart would break.

Then she saw a hair. It was red. It was long. It was silky.

"This hair belongs to Felix Fox!" she cried. "That wicked fox has stolen my egg! I must go and find him, and make him give it back!"

Harriet ran down the street as fast as she could go. On the way, she met Polly Pig.

"Where are you going in such a hurry?" asked the pig.

"The fox has stolen my egg!" cried
Harriet Hen. "I am going to find him, and
make him give it back!"

"I will go with you," grunted Polly.

So they ran down the street as fast as their feet could go. On the way, they met Gussie Goose.

"Where are you going in such a hurry?" asked the goose.

"The fox has stolen my egg!" cried Harriet Hen. "We are going to find him, and make him give it back!"

"I will go with you," honked Gussie.

So they ran down the street as fast as they could go. On the way, they met Harvey Horse.

"Where are you going in such a hurry?" asked the horse.

"The fox has stolen my egg!" cried Harriet Hen. "We are going to find him, and make him give it back!"

"I will go with you," neighed Harvey.
"Jump on my back. I will take you there.
Hold onto my mane, and we will fly like the
wind!"

Up jumped Harriet.
Up jumped Polly.
Up jumped Gussie.
They were soon at the house of Felix
Fox.

Harriet knocked on the door. "Let us in!" she clucked. "We have come for my egg!"

The door opened. "Come in," said Felix Fox.

Into the house of Felix Fox marched Harriet Hen, Polly Pig, Gussie Goose, and Harvey Horse.

"Give me my egg!" demanded Harriet.

"I do not have it," answered the fox.

Harriet flew at the fox, and pecked at his head.

"Hold on!" cried the fox, and he told this story:

"I had the egg. I was about to make an omelet when, suddenly, the egg cracked open and a baby chick hopped out. Yum, said I. I will have fried chicken instead! But before I could reach for the frying pan, in crept Kitty Cat. She stole the chick from under my nose, and ran off with it. And that," said Felix the Fox, "is the truth."

"Then we must find her!" cried Harriet. "We must find Kitty Cat, and make her give back my chick!"

So the hen and the pig and the goose and the horse all galloped off to Kitty Cat's house.

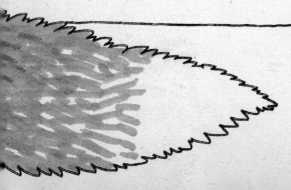

Harriet knocked on the door.
"Give me my chick!" she demanded.
"He is not here," mewed Kitty Cat, and licked her fine whiskers.

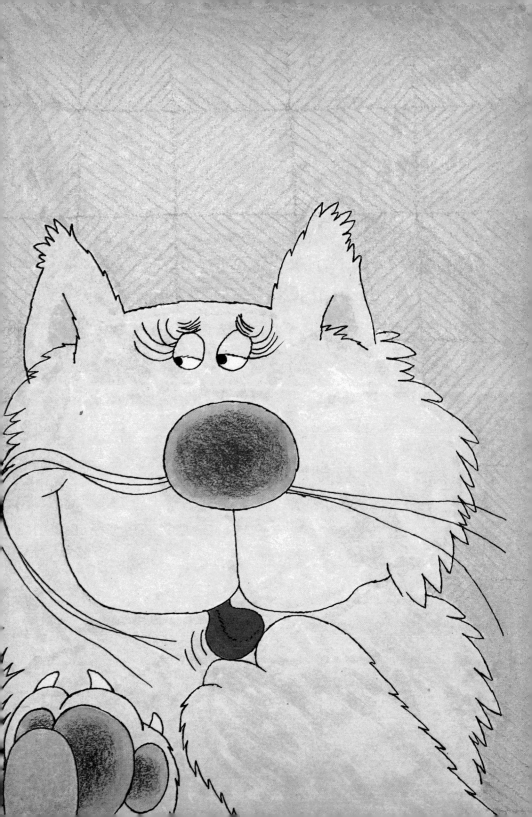

Harriet flew at the cat, and pecked at her head.

"Hold on!" cried Kitty Cat, and she told this story:

"I was running down the street with the chick in my mouth, when Oliver Owl swooped down from the sky. Before I could blink my eyes, he stole the chick and flew away. And that," said Kitty, with a flick of her tail, "is the truth."

"Hurry!" squawked Harriet. "We must find Oliver Owl, and make him give back my chick!"

So the hen and the pig and the goose and the horse all galloped off to Oliver's house.

Harriet knocked on the door.

"Give me my chick!" she demanded.

"He is not here," hooted the owl. He ruffled his feathers and blinked his eyes.

Harriet flew at the owl, and pecked at his head.

"Hold on!" screeched the owl, and he told this story:

"I was on my way home, when I saw Kitty Cat with a mouse in her mouth. I swooped down and stole it away. A nice, plump mouse was just what I wanted for supper. Imagine my surprise when I discovered I had taken, not a mouse, but a baby chick! Well, I had my heart set on a mouse, so I left the chick in Lonesome Wood. Then I came home," said Oliver Owl. "And that's the truth."

Faster than the wind, the four friends galloped to Lonesome Wood.

"We will never find him in this great wood," cried Harriet Hen.

"There, there," honked Gussie Goose. "The wood is big and green. The chick is small and yellow. We will look for something small and yellow in this big green wood. We will look everywhere."

Polly Pig went to the south. She looked and she looked. She saw some ferns. She saw a beetle. Then she saw something small and yellow.

"Come quickly!" she grunted. "I have found the chick!"

But when Harriet and Gussie and Harvey looked, all they saw was a patch of yellow dandelions.

"I am sorry," said Polly. "I thought it was the chick."

Gussie Goose went to the east. She looked and she looked. She saw some toadstools. She saw a spider's web. Then she saw something small and yellow.

"Come quickly!" she honked. "I have found the chick!"

But when Harriet and Polly and Harvey looked, all they saw was a bed of yellow buttercups.

"I am sorry," said Gussie. "I thought it was the chick."

Harvey Horse went to the north. He looked and he looked. He saw some pine cones. He saw a toad. Then he saw something small and yellow.

"Come quickly!" he neighed. "I have found the chick!"

But when Harriet and Gussie and Polly looked, all they saw was a clump of yellow touch-me-nots.

"I am sorry," said Harvey. "I thought it was the chick."

Harriet Hen went to the west. She looked and she looked. She saw some chipmunks. She saw a caterpillar. Then she saw something small and yellow.

"It is only a dandelion or a buttercup or a touch-me-not," said Harriet. "It cannot be my baby chick."

Then the small, yellow something stood
up. It opened its mouth. "Are you my
Mother?" it peeped.

"Everybody come quickly!" cried
Harriet. "I have found my chick!"

Then Polly and Gussie and Harriet, with
her chick held safe in her wings, jumped on
Harvey's back.

"Home, Harvey, Home!"

Then they all went home, faster than the
wind.